CONTENTS

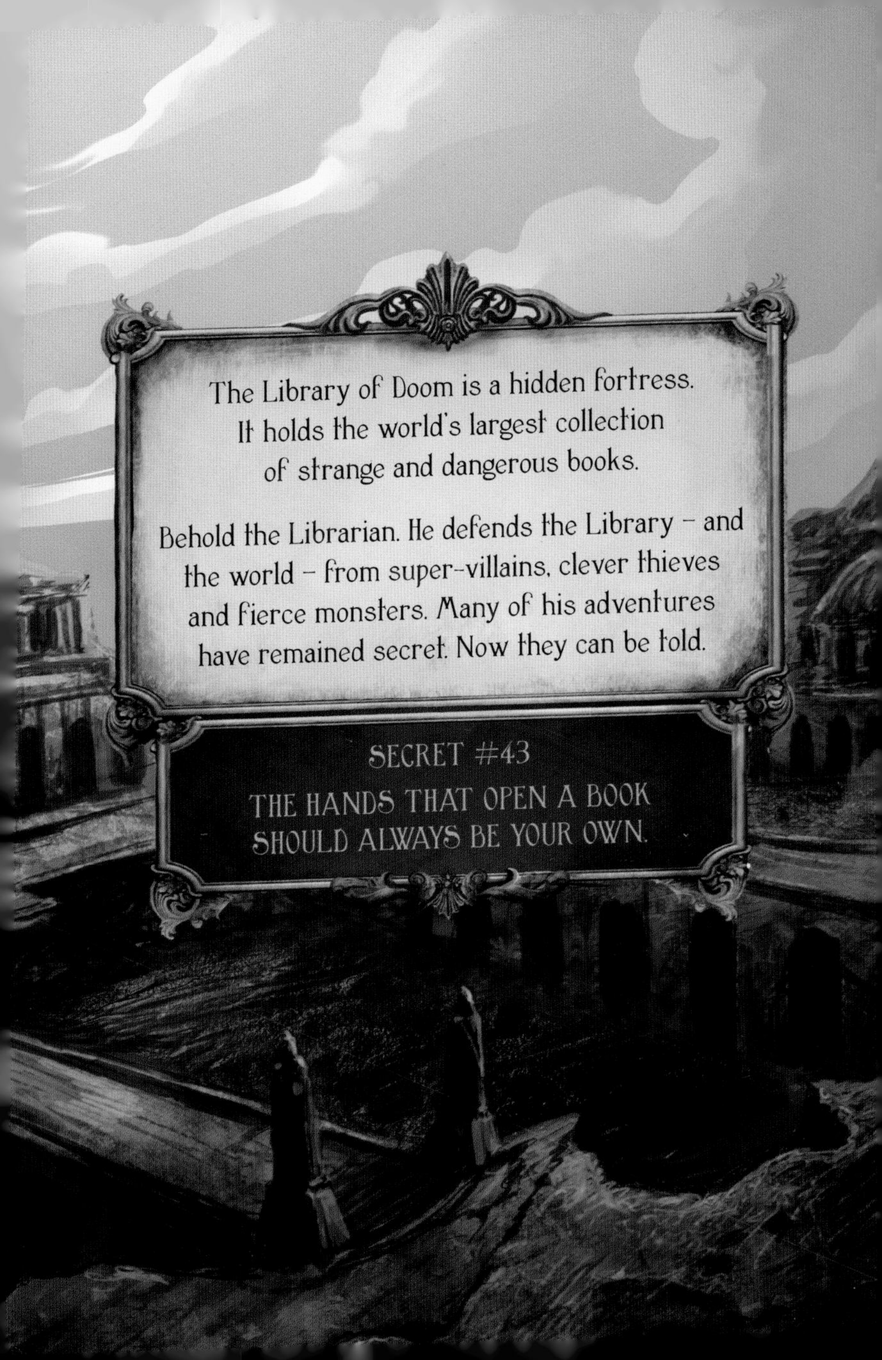
The Library of Doom is a hidden fortress. It holds the world's largest collection of strange and dangerous books.
Behold the Librarian. He defends the Library – and the world – from super-villains, clever thieves and fierce monsters. Many of his adventures have remained secret. Now they can be told.
SECRET #43
THE HANDS THAT OPEN A BOOK SHOULD ALWAYS BE YOUR OWN.

Chapter One

THE TALL WOMAN

Mara walks out of the town library empty-handed. The book she wanted has already been taken out.

She sees a **TALL** figure standing at the bottom of the library's steep stairs. It is a woman dressed in strange clothes.

The woman's hands are **RED**.

As Mara **WALKS** closer, she sees the tall woman is wearing red gloves.

The woman is handing out something to people on the path. They are beautiful BOOKMARKS.

The woman hands one to Mara.

"But I haven't got a book," says the girl.

"You don't need one," the woman says. "Anyway, the bookmark is **FREE**."

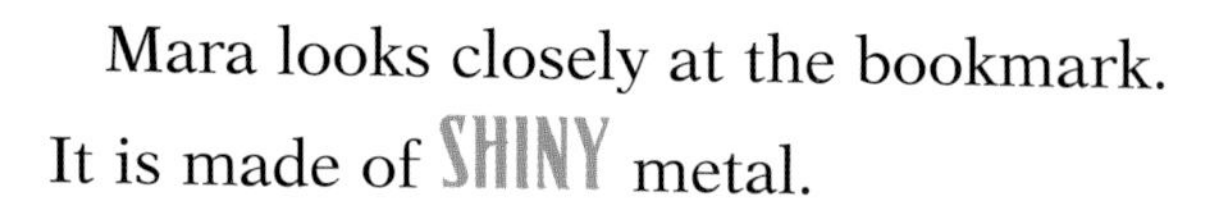

Mara looks closely at the bookmark. It is made of SHINY metal.

The girl touches the **STRANGE** symbols carved on the bookmark.

"Ouch!" Mara cries.

She has CUT her finger on a sharp corner.

The **TALL** woman licks her lips.

"You must be more careful, dear," says the woman.

Chapter Two

BLOOD ON THE BOOKMARK

Mara examines her fingertip.

"It's only a small cut," she says.

PLOP PLOP

One drop of blood FALLS onto the ground.

But another **DROP** falls onto the bookmark.

The blood sinks into the bookmark. The metal starts to turn **RED**.

"What is going on?" asks Mara.

She looks up, but the **TALL** woman is gone.

Mara looks back at the BOOKMARK. It is no longer red.

The metal **SHINES** in Mara's eyes.

The girl does not remember that it **CHANGED** colour just a second ago.

"It is very beautiful," she says to herself.

Mara puts the bookmark in her rucksack and **WALKS** to the bus stop.

She does not see the **TALL** woman watching her.

After Mara has left, the woman steps out of the SHADOWS.

She kneels down and reaches out a RED fingertip.

She touches the drop of blood on the ground.

Then the TALL woman smiles with sharp, white teeth.

Chapter Three

THE BOOK CLUB

It is late afternoon when Mara gets home.

The sky is now **DARK** and cloudy.

The house is QUIET. The girl's mother is still at work.

Mara walks into her bedroom. She sees the metal BOOKMARK lying on her bed.

I must be dreaming, thinks Mara. *The bookmark is in my bag.*

Mara notices a dark shadow **STANDING** outside her window.

It is the **TALL** woman.

The woman takes off her **RED** gloves.

She **SCRATCHES** a long, sharp fingernail against Mara's window.

KRRRRRRKKKKKKK

Mara can see other figures **FLOATING** behind the woman.

They are other young people who took the woman's bookmarks.

Each figure holds a **RED** bookmark.

Each one smiles with **SHARP**, white teeth.

"Open the window," they all say.

"Join us, Mara," says the tall woman. "Join my special book club."

Chapter Four

MARKED!

Mara quickly **SHAKES** her head.

"It's too late," says the woman. "Look at your finger."

Mara glances at the finger that was **CUT**.

STRANGE lines have appeared on her finger and hand.

They are the same lines that are on the BOOKMARK.

"You are marked," says the TALL woman. "That is what led me here."

"You are special, like all my readers," the woman adds. She smiles again. "I will choose a book for you and slip you inside like a bookmark."

Mara backs AWAY from the window.

"You will be SAFE in the book," says the tall woman.

"Safe and sound forever . . . ," say the figures floating behind her.

"No, no, no!" Mara SHOUTS. "You can't put me inside a book!"

The tall woman SCRATCHES on the window with both hands.

KRRRRRRRRKKKKKKKK!!!

The woman stares **ANGRILY** through the glass.

"You must come with me!" she snarls. "I have your special book all picked out!"

Chapter Five

CHOOSE YOUR OWN

Mara grabs the metal BOOKMARK off the bed.

"Take the bookmark back!" she cries. "I don't want it!"

"Open the window, dear," says the tall woman. "Your book is **WAITING** for you."

"I don't want any book you've chosen for me!" shouts Mara.

"But the book is warm and quiet," says the woman. "You will sleep inside forever."

Suddenly a **LOUD** sound fills the room. The sound makes Mara think of a thousand pages being turned.

FF-FF-FF-FF-FF-FF-FF

A man appears in the room. He wears **DARK** glasses and a long jacket.

"Books should wake us up," the man says. "Not put us to sleep!"

"Librarian!" **YELLS** the tall woman.

"Besides," adds the hero, "a good librarian lets the *reader* choose their book."

He raises an arm. The window flies open.

A brilliant light suddenly **BURSTS** from the Librarian's hand.

Mara closes her eyes.

When Mara OPENS her eyes again, the tall woman and her book club have vanished.

The weather outside has turned to BRIGHT sunshine.

The BOOKMARK has also vanished from Mara's hand.

Instead, Mara is holding the book she wanted to get at the library.

The LIBRARIAN smiles at the girl.
"Choose your *own* adventure," he says.

"This is what I choose," says Mara.

She **OPENS** the book.

GLOSSARY

carve cut into a surface to make a pattern or design

examine look at something closely and carefully

figure shape or outline of something, especially a person

float stay or move in the air above the ground

glance look quickly at something

slip move easily and smoothly

steep having a sharp rise or fall, such as on a hill or stairs

symbol letter, picture or sign that stands for something or has a certain meaning

vanish go away completely and suddenly

TALK ABOUT IT

1. At the start of the story, how does the author hint that the tall woman is up to no good? Go back to the beginning and find at least two clues.

2. What sort of books do you choose most often from the library? What do you like about them?

WRITE ABOUT IT

1. Mara is safe, but the tall woman still has other readers under her control! Write a new adventure about how the Librarian rescues them.

2. Most book clubs aren't run by evil beings. Instead, they can be a fun way to read with others. Would you ever join one? Write a paragraph explaining your choice.

ABOUT THE AUTHOR

Michael Dahl is an award-winning author of more than 200 books for young people. He especially likes to write scary or weird fiction. His latest series are the sci-fi adventure Escape from Planet Alcatraz and School Bus of Horrors. As a child, Michael spent lots of time in libraries. "The creepier, the better," he says. These days, besides writing, he likes travelling and hunting for the one, true door that leads to the Library of Doom.

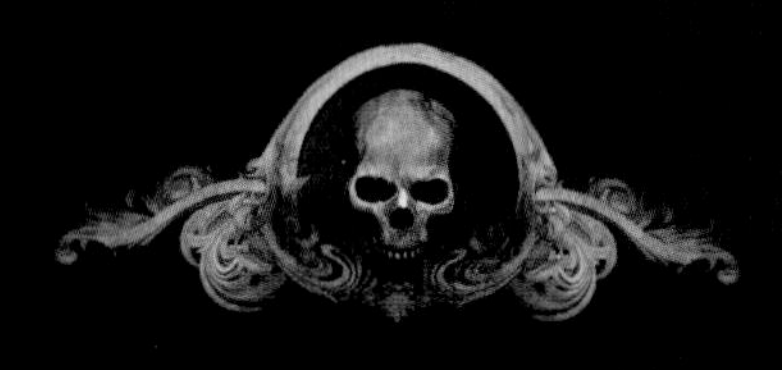

ABOUT THE ILLUSTRATOR

Patricio Clarey was born in Argentina. He graduated in fine arts from the Martín A. Malharro School of Visual Arts, specializing in illustration and graphic design. Patricio currently lives in Barcelona, Spain, where he works as a freelance graphic designer and illustrator. He has created several comics and graphic novels, and his work has been featured in books and other publications.